Barbie™

A Day with the Pet Doctor

By Katherine Poindexter

 A GOLDEN BOOK • NEW YORK

Golden Books Publishing Company, Inc.,
New York, New York 10106

Courtney was so excited! Dr. Barbie had invited her to spend the day at her animal clinic. Courtney thought she might like to be a pet doctor, too, one day.

"How did you know you wanted to be a pet doctor?" Courtney asked as Barbie drove them to the clinic.

"I've always loved animals," Barbie said. "When I was in the fourth grade, I guessed how many marbles were in a jar and won a contest. Guess what I won?"

"A book about animals?" Courtney guessed.

"Even better!" Barbie said. "A kitten! I named her Cuddles. She was my very first pet." Barbie grinned. "Maybe that was when it all began."

At Barbie's animal clinic, Courtney was amazed to see all kinds of animals—dogs, cats, birds, even a rabbit! "I guess being a pet doctor is almost like having dozens of pets!" she exclaimed.

"In a way," Dr. Barbie agreed. "But they only stay here until they get well."

Just then, a girl named Megan hurried into the office. She was carrying a big box with a beautiful black cat inside.

"Oh, Dr. Barbie!" she cried. "I'm really worried about Midnight. She's been acting strange and meowing a lot. And her tummy's swollen. Do you think she has a stomachache?"

Dr. Barbie led the two girls into an examining room. Then she gently lifted Midnight out of the box and placed her on the table.

Courtney and Megan watched Dr. Barbie examine the meowing cat.

"Don't worry, Megan," Dr. Barbie said at last with a reassuring smile. "I think I know what's wrong with Midnight."

Courtney and Megan looked at each other. What could be wrong with Midnight that would make Dr. Barbie smile?

"Why don't you leave Midnight here for a few hours?" Dr. Barbie said. "Come back at around noon."

"Okay," Megan said, trying not to worry.

Courtney watched as Barbie examined her next patient. It was a little dog who barked happily and wagged its tail.

"I'm glad to see you again, too, Rascal!" Dr. Barbie said, patting the dog.

"Rascal doesn't look sick to me," Courtney said.

"Not all animals who come to see me are hurt or sick," Dr. Barbie explained. "Just like people, animals need checkups to stay healthy." Barbie gave Rascal his vaccinations—shots to keep him from getting sick.

"I had to get shots from my doctor when I started school," Courtney said.

"Right, just like Rascal," said Dr. Barbie. "See his tags?"

Courtney nodded. "I know what they're for. They show that he's had his shots. And this one has his name and address—in case he ever gets lost."

Barbie checked on several more animals. Then she picked up her medical kit and headed for the door. "Come on, Courtney," she said.

Courtney was disappointed. "Do I have to go home already?" she asked.

Barbie laughed. "Of course not! But not all my patients can come to my office. So we have to go see them."

"You mean some poor animal is so sick it can't even come to the office?" Courtney said, worried.

"Not too sick," Barbie answered. "Just too big!"

When Barbie drove up to a nearby farm, Courtney saw what Barbie meant. "A horse!" Courtney cried.

The farm's owner, Mr. Greene, and his daughter Ashley were leading a horse out of the barn.

"Stardancer cut her nose trying to open her stall," Ashley explained as Dr. Barbie and Courtney approached them.

Barbie examined the horse. "It's not too serious," she said. Then she turned to Stardancer. "But you'll have to be good and keep that cut clean until it heals," she told the horse.

Courtney and Ashley laughed. "But Barbie," Courtney wondered aloud, "how do you get a horse to wash its face?"

"I have a trick," Barbie explained. She and the girls filled a big bucket with clean water. "Now we add something special."

"Medicine?" Courtney guessed.

"No—apples!" Barbie said with a laugh.

"That's Stardancer's favorite treat!" Ashley cried.

Ashley ran to get some apples. Sure enough, Stardancer was more than happy to dunk her nose into the bucket of clean water to bob for them!

"Thanks, Dr. Barbie," Ashley said happily.

On the way back to the office, Dr. Barbie had to hit the brakes. A puppy had dashed into the street right in front of her car!

Dr. Barbie got out to make sure the puppy was all right. Then she spoke to the dog's owner.

"It's very important to keep your dog on a leash," she explained, "especially a puppy who hasn't learned to understand and obey your commands."

The boy promised to do as Dr. Barbie said.

When Barbie and Courtney got back to the animal clinic, Barbie checked on the animals in the kennel. "We keep some animals here overnight," she explained. "Some stay until we're sure they're well enough to go home. Others stay here while their owners are away."

"Like a hotel?" Courtney asked.

"Pretty much!" Barbie answered.

DOG FOOD

CAT FOOD

SUPPLIES

TO

EXAM ROOM A

Just as they returned to the waiting room, Megan rushed back into the office. "Oh, Dr. Barbie!" she cried, "I've been so worried about Midnight. Were you able to make her well?"

"She's going to be fine," Dr. Barbie assured her.

"Come on. Let's go see how she's doing. Shhh," Dr. Barbie whispered as she opened the door. "I believe Midnight may have a surprise for you."

Wide-eyed, the girls tiptoed into the room.

"Kittens!" Megan and Courtney exclaimed together.

There was Midnight, resting peacefully with her new kittens snuggled around her.

"How many are there?" Courtney asked quietly.

Megan counted. "One, two, three, four . . . five!" she said. "Aren't they cute! Oh, thank you, Dr. Barbie."

Dr. Barbie smiled.

"The new kittens have to stay with their mother for at least six weeks," Dr. Barbie explained. "You might want to start looking for new homes for them."

"If my mom says it's okay, could I have one?" Courtney asked.

"Sure," said Megan.

"And you didn't even have to guess how many marbles were in a jar like I did!" Dr. Barbie said with a grin.